I, AMBER BROWN, AM DEFINITELY ONE VERY UNHAPPY HUMAN BEING.

To prove that I'm not upset, I repeat Hannah's question. "Any other kids there?"

Justin nods. "Lots. Next door, the family has five kids, two old enough to babysit for Danny, one my age, Jon—they call him Junior—and one Danny's age, Jim Bob."

"Twins?" Tiffany Shroeder asks.

"No." Justin explains. "A lot of people there have two first names."

Great, I think. Next thing, we're going to have to start calling him "Justin Bob."

Justin keeps blabbing on.

I keep waiting for him to mention the very important thing that his new school and neighborhood doesn't have—ME.

But he never does.

To Carrie Marie Danziger:
niece, consultant and pal.

PUFFIN BOOKS
Published by the Penguin Group
Penguin Young Readers Group,
345 Hudson Street, New York, New York 10014, U.S.A.
Penguin Group (Canada), 90 Eglinton Avenue East, Suite 700, Toronto, Ontario, Canada M4P 2Y3
(a division of Pearson Penguin Canada Inc.)
Penguin Books Ltd, 80 Strand, London WC2R 0RL, England
Penguin Ireland, 25 St Stephen's Green, Dublin 2, Ireland (a division of Penguin Books Ltd)
Penguin Group (Australia), 250 Camberwell Road, Camberwell, Victoria 3124, Australia
(a division of Pearson Australia Group Pty Ltd)
Penguin Books India Pvt Ltd, 11 Community Centre, Panchsheel Park, New Delhi - 110 017, India
Penguin Group (NZ), Cnr Airborne and Rosedale Roads, Albany, Auckland 1310, New Zealand
(a division of Pearson New Zealand Ltd)
Penguin Books (South Africa) (Pty) Ltd, 24 Sturdee Avenue,
Rosebank, Johannesburg 2196, South Africa

Registered Offices: Penguin Books Ltd, 80 Strand, London WC2R 0RL, England

First published in the United States of America by G. P. Putnam's Sons,
a division of The Putnam & Grosset Group, 1994
Published by Puffin Books, a division of Penguin Young Readers Group, 2006

9 10

Text copyright © Paula Danziger, 1994
Illustrations copyright © Tony Ross, 1994
All rights reserved.

THE LIBRARY OF CONGRESS HAS CATALOGED THE G. P. PUTNAM'S SONS EDITION AS FOLLOWS:
Danziger, Paula, 1944–2004
Amber Brown is not a crayon / Paula Danziger.
p. cm.
Summary: The year she is in third grade is a sad time for Amber because
her best friend Justin is getting ready to move to a distant state.
ISBN: 0-399-22509-9 (hc)
[1. Friendship—Fiction. 2. Moving, Household—Fiction. 3. Schools—Fiction.] I. Title.
PZ7.D2394Am 1994
[Fic]—dc20 92-34678 CIP AC

Puffin Books ISBN 0-14-240619-8

Printed in the United States of America

Designed by Donna Mark.
Lettering by David Gatti.
Text set in Bembo.

Paula Danziger

Amber Brown is Not a Crayon

Illustrated by Tony Ross

PUFFIN BOOKS

Chapter
One

In just ten minutes, our entire class is getting on a plane for our flight to China.

I, Amber Brown, am one very excited third grader.

My best friend, Justin Daniels, is going to sit next to me.

Right now, he's sitting at the desk next to me, pretending to be an alarm clock.

All I hear now is a quiet tick tock, tick tock, but I'm absolutely positively sure that he has something else planned.

We always sit together when our class flies to some faraway place.

In fact, we've been sitting together since we first met in preschool, but that's another story.

Finding my passport and tickets is not easy because I, Amber Brown, am one very messy third grader.

I quickly pull things out of my desk—the book I'm going to use for my report, half a roll of strawberry licorice, my sticker book, two headbands, seven rubber bands, eleven paper clips, two workbooks, and finally, my passport and tickets, which I have put in a specially decorated case. (I used a lot of my stickers on it.)

"Bzzzzzz. Squawk." Justin starts rocking back and forth.

I hit him on the head with my passport and tickets. "Okay. What are you doing this time?"

"I'm a cuckoo bird alarm clock and my tail feathers are caught." Justin bobs back and forth.

Having Justin Daniels as my best friend sure makes life more fun.

So does having Mr. Cohen as my teacher.

"Get ready to board." Mr. Cohen flicks the lights off and on to signal the end of one activity and the beginning of another.

All of the chairs in the classroom are lined up so that it looks like a real plane, with aisles to walk down and places for the pilot, co-pilot and flight attendants.

Mr. Cohen is always the pilot. He says that's because he's the only one in the room with a driver's license but I know the real reason he's always the pilot. It's because he wants to make sure that we get to where we're supposed to go. Once he let Roger Hart be the pilot, but when we got there, Roger announced that he had taken us to Disneyland instead of Zaire.

So now, Mr. Cohen is the pilot all the time and he picks different kids to be co-pilots and flight attendants. When my turn comes, I want to be co-pilot. I don't want to have to pass out the little packets of peanuts, because some of the boys act so immature, making monkey sounds and stuff.

Not Justin though. He and I spend the time reading the *ROOM 3-B IN FLIGHT* magazine. (Everyone writes articles for it.) We also do the crossword puzzle that Mr. Cohen makes up.

Well, actually, to be honest, sometimes Justin makes monkey sounds, too.

The class lines up, waiting for our passports to be checked by Mr. Cohen.

Hannah Burton looks at the photo on her passport. "I hate this picture of me. I don't know why we couldn't just bring one from home."

Every time we start studying a new country, we "fly" there, and every time we do, Hannah complains about the picture on her passport.

"You look perfectly good," I tell her, looking at her school picture.

We all use our school pictures, except for Brandi Colwin who came to school after the pictures were taken. Her passport has a picture that Mr. Cohen took with his instant camera.

Hannah shakes her head. "I am perfectly good. I just look really terrible in my picture."

I choose to ignore Hannah's correction. "You know that Mr. Cohen wants our make-believe passports to look like the real thing. Remember when he showed us his real passport. It looked awful, and he doesn't really look that bad."

Hannah makes a face and grins. "Amber,

just because you forgot which day the pictures were going to be taken and your picture looks like you jumped out of bed, threw on any old clothes and combed your hair with a rake, doesn't mean that the rest of us don't care about how we look in our photos."

I look at Hannah's picture. Her long blond hair is perfectly combed, with a really pretty multicolored ribbon barrette.

I look at my picture.

Brown eyes, freckled nose. . . . My brown, slightly messy hair is held back with two bagel-shaped barrettes.

I'm wearing normal, nonpicture-taking-day clothes. In fact, I'm wearing my favorite things . . . a very long T-shirt that my aunt Pamela brought back from a trip to London and a pair of black stirrup pants. (Even though it doesn't show, I remember which pants I was wearing. I, Amber Brown, have a very good memory.)

I don't look so bad, and anyway, I forgot that the pictures were being taken that day, even though Mr. Cohen told us a million times, even though he had written two million reminders on the blackboard.

So I'm a little forgetful.

And Hannah Burton isn't always totally right. I don't comb my hair with a rake. Maybe my fingers sometimes but never a rake.

"I like your picture." Justin grins at me. "It looks exactly like you, not just the way you look but the way you act."

"You mean messy." Hannah laughs.

I want to pull off the stupid little bow that she's wearing on her head.

"Don't you dare." Justin pulls on my arm.

I like the way that Justin usually knows what I'm thinking and I usually know what he's thinking.

Mr. Cohen checks our passports, looks at

our boarding tickets, and then Joey Fortunato leads us to our seats.

Once everyone is seated, Joey shows us how to fasten our seatbelts and tells us what to do in case of an emergency.

Mr. Cohen gets on his make-believe microphone and tells us to get ready for the trip of a lifetime.

And off we go—into the wild blue yonder.

The third grade is on its way to China.

Chapter Two

China.

It's a nice place to visit.

Once we got off the plane, Mr. Cohen showed us a film about China and then we worked on our scrapbooks about the trip.

Justin and I are cutting out pictures from the folders that the travel agency sent.

We're turning them into postcards, to make it seem like we're really in China. Then we're writing important facts about the places in the scrapbook.

Justin holds up a picture of a giant panda

and says, "Let's send this to Danny the Bratster."

"You mean, Danny the Bratster, your little brother, the four-year-old you hate sharing your room with." I paste the picture on a notecard.

"The same. The one and only." Justin nods, takes the card and writes:

Having a wonderful time. Glad you're not here. I bearly miss you.

"That's B-A-R-E-L-Y," I inform him.

Justin makes a face. "With the panda, B-E-A-R-L-Y is better. Don't worry. Danny can't read anyway."

"Not your handwriting, at least." I stare at the scribble.

Justin looks down at the card. "I'll do the pasting. You do the cursive."

Looking at the gobs of paste, I think

"messy." If neatness counts, with me the count hardly gets to one.

Justin, on the other hand, is very neat about pasting things.

My handwriting is much better.

Another example of what a great team we are. We help each other out. We also learn things at about the same time, and when one of us learns first, he or she helps the other one out. When I learned to make the "e" go forward, not "ɘ," I taught Justin. He helps me with fractions, which I only half understand. We both whisper words to each other in reading group when we need help—a great team.

Justin keeps pasting.

I keep writing.

We "send" one postcard to Justin's father, who got a new job and has to live alone in Alabama. Justin, Danny and his mother are staying here, in New Jersey, until their house gets sold.

That's taking a long time.

Secretly, I'm glad.

Sometimes Justin gets a little sad.

I'm not glad about that.

I know how Justin feels about missing his father. When my parents got a divorce, my dad moved far away, to another country, so I never get to see him and he hardly ever calls. Justin's lucky though. His father comes home some weekends, and he gets to talk to him a lot on the phone.

And even though Justin misses his dad, I keep my fingers crossed a lot of the time hoping that no one buys their house and that Mr. Daniels gets a job here and moves back again.

At the other end of the table, Jimmy Russell and Bobby Clifford are fighting.

"Listen, tuna head, I need the brown crayon." Jimmy tugs at Bobby's sleeve. "I've asked you for it forty-seven times."

"And forty-seven times, I've told you

that I still need it, rat rear." Bobby keeps using the crayon. "Why don't you just use another color?"

"Because I need brown." Jimmy throws down a blue crayon.

Jimmy and Bobby have been fighting since preschool.

Mr. Cohen has told them to "grow out of it," but they haven't.

"Brown. I need brown," Jimmy repeats.

Bobby crosses his eyes, sticks out his tongue and clutches the brown crayon to his chest.

"Doofus." Jimmy wiggles his ears.

"If you need a brown crayon," Bobby points to me, "why don't you use the top of her head. She's amber brown."

I stare at Bobby. "Amber Brown is not a crayon. Amber Brown is a person."

The two boys laugh.

I, Amber Brown, am so sick of people teasing me about my name. When I was younger, I used to wish that my parents had given me a normal name like Jennifer or Tiffany or Chelsea.

Now, though, I really like my name.

But I still have to put up with goofballs teasing me about it.

Mr. Cohen flicks the lights off and on. "Lunchtime in China. Clear the desks."

Everyone quickly cleans up.

I see Bobby put the brown crayon in his pocket for later.

In walk Ms. Armitage, Mr. Burton and Mrs. Hopkins.

The classroom parents committee brings in Chinese takeout food and we start eating "in" China, not "on" china because we're using paper plates.

I, Amber Brown, am not very good with chopsticks. I use mine to spear the food and then use a fork for the rice.

After we finish eating, Justin and I fence with our chopsticks.

Then Mr. Cohen passes out the fortune
cookies.

Opening mine up, I read:

Experience is the Best Teacher.

I hold the paper up and show it to Mr. Cohen. "I thought YOU were the best teacher. Who is Mr. Experience?"

Mr. Cohen grins and then heads off to settle a fight between Jimmy and Bobby.

Justin has put his fortune down on the desk in front of him.

He stares at the blackboard.

I pick it up.

It says:

> Soon you will be going on a new
> journey and beginning a new life.

I put the fortune down.

Suddenly, I don't feel very good.

Suddenly, pieces of dry fortune cookie feel like they are choking me.

I, Amber Brown, hope that the fortune cookies are wrong.

Chapter Three

"Snack time." Justin puts the package of Oreos on his kitchen table.

"Yum." I rip the package open, take out a cookie, eat the cream center out of the middle and hand the cookie parts to Justin.

"Yum." He eats them.

I take a second cookie and eat the center out of it.

Justin and I have been eating cookies like this since preschool.

We call it teamwork.

Hannah Burton calls it "gross."

Mrs. Daniels walks into the kitchen.

Danny follows. "Play Legos with me."

"Leg. Legos. What's the difference?" Justin walks over to his brother and pulls at his leg.

I wish I had a little brother or sister to tease. Being an only child means I don't, but it's okay, I guess, because I can always tease Danny.

Mrs. Daniels tells Danny, "You can play with your toys later. Right now I don't want you to make a mess because the real estate broker is bringing people over to look at the house."

Suddenly, teasing Danny doesn't seem so important. Suddenly, it's much more important to cross my fingers and wish very hard—very, very hard. I wish that the people hate the house, that they think it's too big or too small, that they don't have the money to buy it.

The doorbell rings.

"Would you two play with Danny?"

Mrs. Daniels asks and then leaves to answer the door.

"Cookie." Danny imitates the sound of the Cookie Monster on *Sesame Street*.

"Sure, Walter." I hand him a cookie.

Walter is Danny's real name but when he was little he had trouble saying it and kept calling himself "Danny Danny."

The name stuck and now everyone calls him Danny, except for Justin and me when we want to torment him.

Danny starts to sing a song. "Amber Brown is a crayon . . . a crayon . . . a crayon . . . a broken old crayon."

Something tells me that I never should have let him know how I hate the way that some kids tease me about my name.

I guess that it's probably not such a good idea to tease someone about a name when they can tease back.

We all eat a few more cookies and then

take a plastic bowl and start throwing cookies into it.

"Two points. Yes!" I yell, as my cookie
rims the bowl and falls in.

"Good shot," a strange voice says.

Looking up, I see a very pregnant lady
who applauds my athletic ability.

"Maybe Amber should try out for the
gold medal in the cookie Olympics." Justin
grins.

"Maybe you kids should play in another
room while Mrs. Bradley looks at the
kitchen." Mrs. Daniels smiles and motions
us out.

"It's all right. I like seeing children in the
kitchen. I've already got a four-year-old."
Mrs. Bradley pats her stomach. "And this
one will be here in a few months. So I like
the idea of a kitchen with children playing
in it." She looks around.

I debate telling her that there are dragons

in the basement, ghosts in the walls, and ectoplasm in the attic.

"You've done a really nice job decorating." Mrs. Bradley is looking in a cupboard, which has shelves that twirl around.

"Thank you," Mrs. Daniels says. "We've really loved living here and hope that the next family loves it, too."

I don't want there to be a "next family" here.

I remember how we all sat around looking at wallpaper and stuff when the kitchen was being redone.

Mrs. Daniels said that since everyone in the house was going to see it every day, everyone could help decorate it. She also said that since I was practically a member of the family, I could help, too.

They didn't pick the wallpaper that Justin and I wanted, baseball players.

Instead, there are flowers all over the wall.

Mrs. Bradley says, "If you don't mind, I would like my husband to see this house soon."

Soon. That sounds serious.

I can't help myself. "I hope you don't mind alligators in the toilet."

Mrs. Bradley looks surprised and then she grins. "Alligators in the toilet. That's quite a bonus."

She and Mrs. Daniels look at each other and smile.

This is definitely not a good sign.

The grown-ups leave the room.

Justin, Danny and I continue playing cookie basketball.

We pretend that everything's the same.

I try not to get too nervous. After all, a zillion people have seen the house and not bought it.

Maybe Mrs. Bradley's husband will hate it. I hope I'm here when he looks at the house. I'll be sure to mention giant termites.

Mrs. Daniel returns.

"Amber, would you like to stay for dinner tonight? I'll call your mother and see if she wants to join us. We'll order pizza."

"Yes," I say, feeling a little better.

This is something we do a lot, especially since my parents got a divorce.

I stay with the Danielses until my mom gets home from work and then sometimes we all eat together. Pizza is Justin's and my favorite food group.

Mrs. Daniels gets on the phone.

My mother says yes.

Then Mrs. Daniels calls the pizza place. "Extra cheese, mushrooms, and sausage, please."

Justin and I yell at the same time, "And hold the anchovies."

Then we laugh, imagining what the guy looks like holding the anchovies.

And for a while, I forget that the house might get sold.

Chapter Four

"Ka-thwonk. Ka-thwonk. Ka-thwonk." Justin hops up and down as we walk out of the school.

I'm in a very good mood. I know that my finger crossing has worked because they haven't heard from Mrs. Bradley.

I pretend that he's acting perfectly normal. "So, Justin, what book are you doing for your report?"

"Ka-thwonk. Ka-thwonk. Ka-thwonk." He hops around me, making a circle.

"I've never read that book. Who wrote

it?" I tease him, trying to look him in the eye.

That's not easy when someone is jumping up and down all around you.

For two more blocks, we walk along. I talk. Justin ka-thwonks and talks.

"I'm going to read *Charlotte's Web* and then do a diorama." I skip along.

"Diorama sounds like a disease that a boy sheep gets—Die...O...Ram...a. Ka-thwonk.

Ka-thwonk." Justin hops around me.

I try to step on his foot. "You're acting so silly. You know we made dioramas when we did our reports on the pioneers. Stop hopping and talk to me."

"Ka-thwonk. Ka-thwonk." He jumps too fast for me to get him.

"Enough already." I yell. "Stop that. You're driving me crazy. WHAT are you doing?"

He stands still. "I'm practicing being a kangaroo to get ready for our trip to Australia. Mr. Cohen says that we have three weeks before we go."

"You're not planning on being a kangaroo for three more weeks, are you?" I shake my head. "Justin, sometimes you really are a nut case."

Justin walks over to a tree and picks up a leaf from the ground. "No, actually I am planning to be a koala for part of the time."

"Don't." I yell, just as he chews on a leaf.

Grinning, he puts a little more in his mouth.

"Justin Daniels. Stop that." I shake my finger at him. "You don't know what yucky bug has slithered on that leaf, or what bird has dropped something on it, or . . ."

"Stop." Justin spits out the bits of leaf in his mouth.

I can't seem to stop myself. I, Amber

Brown, have what Mr. Cohen calls "an active imagination."

"Or what dog came by while the leaf was on the ground . . ."

"That's disgusting." He makes a face.

I take a bow and continue. "Or if you're eating poison ivy, or if you'll catch Dutch elm disease, or whatever it was that my mom said our tree had."

Justin shakes his head. "Amber Brown. You are such a worry wart."

"I'm so worried that you just said that." I stick my tongue out at him.

He twitches his nose and sticks his tongue out at me.

I wiggle my ears, twitch my nose and stick out my tongue at him.

Hannah Burton and Brandi Colwin walk past us.

We can hear Hannah say, "How immature."

"Thank you." We both yell at the same time and bow.

"SOOOOOO immature." Hannah shakes her head.

Brandi grins at us and waves as they walk down the block.

"Ka-thwonk. Ka-thwonk." Justin looks at me. "Want to race?"

"Sure." I stand next to him. "On your mark . . . get set . . . hop."

We hop all the way to his house.

"I win!" I yell as I get to the front of his house first.

Justin stops hopping.

I repeat. "I win. You know the rules. You have to say, 'You win,' and then you have to burp. Come on. You know that's the way we always do it."

He's not saying anything.

He's not burping.

He just keeps staring at something on his front lawn.

I turn to see what he's staring at.

The FOR SALE sign on his front lawn has been covered by a SOLD sticker.

All of a sudden, I don't feel very much like a winner.

Chapter Five

"So where's your boyfriend?" Jimmy comes up to my desk on Wednesday morning and teases me. "How come he hasn't been in school for three days? Did he get sick of you?"

"Leave her alone," Brandi tells him. "You're being so mean. Mr. Cohen told you that Justin and his mom and brother flew to see Mr. Daniels and to look for a new house."

I chew on a strand of my hair. "They got back real late last night. It was foggy or something and they couldn't land right away and then they missed a connection or something and they didn't get in until three in the morning. That's what Mrs. Daniels told my mom when we called her this morning. She said that they were going to try to get some sleep."

"Wow. That sounds SO exciting," Brandi says. "Their trip, I mean, not the going-to-sleep part."

"Yea. Exciting," I say, in what my mother calls "Little Ms. Amber's sarcastic voice." Justin got to go on a REAL plane before I did. Life sure isn't fair some days . . . some years.

Mr. Cohen flicks the lights off and on. "Continue working on your China project."

I reach into the desk and pull out half of a peanut butter and M&M sandwich. I made it one day when my mother overslept and asked me to make my own lunch.

When I look at the sandwich, I think

about the joke that Justin told me before he went away . . . about the person so dumb that he got fired from his job at the M&M factory for throwing away every piece of candy with a "W" on it.

I find the scrapbook under an overdue library book.

Looking through it, I realize that there's a chance that Justin won't even be here to finish it. Soon I may even be sending postcards to him.

I try working on the scrapbook, but it's no use. I can't. I'm too sad.

When I grow up and remember third grade, I'm going to immediately try to forget it.

This is definitely the worst year of my life . . . the very, very, very, very worst.

I thought it couldn't get worse when my parents started fighting more than usual.

I thought it couldn't get worse when my parents sat down with me at the kitchen table and told me that they were going to get a divorce.

For a long time after that, I felt sick to my stomach every time I sat down at that table.

I thought the year couldn't get any worse when my father told me that his company was moving him to France for at least a year.

Things were just getting a little better and then I found out that Justin's father got a great new job.

Justin and I begged him not to take it. Justin even offered to take a cut in his allowance. I even offered to give Mr. Daniels part of mine.

But no, he took the job. He said that it was an offer he couldn't refuse, that it was a great promotion with lots more money.

I think that one of the worst days of my life was when the real estate lady put the FOR SALE sign on the Danielses' lawn.

But then things got better, because months went by and no one bought it.

I did feel a little guilty being so happy that the house wasn't sold but, to be absolutely honest, not all that guilty.

And now it's happened.

Mrs. Bradley saw the house and wanted it. Then Mr. Bradley saw it and he wanted it, too, and they bought it.

I was positive that the day two weeks ago when we saw the SOLD sticker on the sign was the worst day of my life.

But that was only the beginning of worst days.

Justin and his mom have been so busy they haven't even had much time for me.

Even though I still go over there, Mrs. Daniels is always packing.

And Justin will play, but he won't talk about how they really are leaving.

I feel so sad just thinking about Justin leaving and try to think of something good about his going. (My mom always tells me to try to find at least one good thing in even a bad time.)

It takes a long while to think of one good thing, and then it comes to me.

When Justin leaves, I can store some of my stuff in his desk. That way I won't have to clean up my desk.

As messy as I, Amber Brown, am, I would clean up my desk every day if only Justin could stay.

I try to think of other reasons to be glad

that Justin is leaving, and I can't think of one.

Justin's being gone for the entire weekend plus two school days let me see what it's going to be like when he really does leave.

And I really don't like what I'm seeing . . . or what I'm feeling.

I, Amber Brown, am definitely one very unhappy human being.

Chapter Six

I'm halfway through a worksheet on fractions when Justin walks into class.

I'm so glad, not only that he's back but that he can help me to understand what to do with $\frac{4}{6} = \frac{2}{3}$.

He sits down at his desk.

I hand him the box of wooden fraction pieces. "Welcome back."

He smiles and then looks over at my worksheet. "The answer is '4.'"

Mr. Cohen comes over, hands him a worksheet and says, "Welcome back. How's it going?"

"Great." Justin reaches into his knapsack and pulls out a pencil with Alabama written on it. "This is for your collection, Mr. Cohen."

Great? Great? Great, I think. Here I spent all of this time missing him and he says things are going great.

Justin smiles. "A lot happened."

Leaning down, Mr. Cohen quietly asks Justin, "Later, would you like to tell the class about what's happening? You certainly don't have to, but if you want to, it might be fun to share."

"Sure." Justin nods.

As Mr. Cohen walks away, I wish that he hadn't said that to Justin. I want Justin to tell me first, not to have everyone find out at the same time.

I look over at Justin.

He is doing the math work very quickly.

I look down at my math and then start chewing on my stub of a pencil.

It would have been nice if Justin had given me a new pencil, too.

Finished with his math, Justin picks up my paper and checks it out.

He finds two mistakes, shows me how to do it correctly and then helps me finish up.

Fractions are not my favorite thing.

In fact, they are one of my least favorite things. The only things I hate more are 1) Brussels sprouts, 2) watching kids pick their noses and eat the snot and 3) having people I love leave.

Mr. Cohen flicks the lights off and on. "Take a minute to finish the problem you're working on and raise your hand if you want me to come over and explain anything. You can finish this up for homework."

People finish up.

Since Justin and I are already done, we play tic-tac-toe.

I win.

We enter the win on a scorecard that Justin keeps in his desk.

We've been keeping track since the beginning of the school year.

I'm ahead. Two hundred and twenty to one hundred and ninety-nine.

The lights flick off and on.

"Clear your desks. Get ready to pay attention. Justin is going to tell us about his trip."

Everyone gets ready, and Justin goes to the front of the room.

I'm sure that he's not going to tell them everything, that there will be some stuff that he'll just tell me.

Justin begins. "We left very early on Saturday morning."

He's wearing a brand-new sweatshirt, one that says "Alabama."

Personally, I don't like the sweatshirt.

I wish he had on a sweatshirt that I know.

He continues, "The airplane trip was really fun. Before the plane took off, the flight attendant let me go up front and see the cockpit and meet the pilot. They gave me wings to wear."

"Like an angel," Jimmy calls out. "So where's your halo?"

"Jimmy." Mr. Cohen uses his teacher "cut it out" voice.

"Wings." Justin points to the pin on his sweatshirt. "And then we sat down and the plane went up and this lady in front of us threw up into the barf bag. . . ."

"Ewwww," "yug," "gross" and "yea" are a few of the comments from the class.

The comment from Mr. Cohen is "Justin. Continue, please—without all the gory details."

Justin continues.

He talks about meeting his dad at the airport, about the motel they stayed at, with a game room, swimming pool, room service and everything.

Then he tells us how Mr. Daniels had been looking at lots of houses, and they all went around to check out the ones he liked best.

And they found one that they all liked.

They picked it out the first day.

I thought buying a house was supposed to take a long, long time.

Justin tells us how big the house is, how he and Danny are going to have their own rooms, how his mom said that he could put up baseball player wallpaper in his room and how there was a special area in the backyard with a basketball hoop.

"Any other kids there?" Hannah asks.

Brandi gives Hannah's arm a shove.

"What's that for?" Hannah rubs her arm as if she'd been run over by a bulldozer. "I just asked a simple question."

Brandi looks over at me.

I stare ahead as if nothing's bothering me.

To prove that I'm not upset, I repeat Hannah's question. "Any other kids there?"

Justin nods. "Lots. Next door, the family has five kids, two old enough to babysit for Danny, one my age, Jon—they call him

Junior—and one Danny's age, Jim Bob."

"Twins?" Tiffany Shroeder asks.

"No." Justin explains. "A lot of people there have two first names.

Great, I think. Next thing, we're going to have to start calling him "Justin Bob."

Justin goes on.

He tells us about the university where his dad works, how there's a great game room there and how there's lots of stuff to do.

Then he tells us about the school they visited, the school that is going to be his NEW school.

He goes on about how they not only have desks, but they have their own lockers, about how it was just built a few years ago, about how instead of just one third grade like we have at our school there are four third grades, how you don't have to bring your own lunch because there's a cafeteria that serves complete meals, how the school even has air conditioning.

Justin keeps blabbing on.

I keep waiting for him to mention the very important thing that his new school and neighborhood doesn't have—ME.

But he never does.

Chapter Seven

The Danielses' house looks like a cyclone hit it, then a tornado, followed by an earthquake and finally a meteor fell on it.

"What a dump." Mrs. Daniels looks around her kitchen.

There's stuff all over the place. Pots. Pans. Dishes. Boxes of food. Spices.

The place is a real mess, kind of like my bedroom usually looks but not at all like the Danielses' house looks normally.

But I guess there's no more "normal" because everything's getting packed.

Mrs. Daniels sighs. "Kids. Please stay out

of my way. We've got to be out of here in two and a half weeks."

I wish I didn't even have to be here right now but my mother had to go to work for a couple of hours, even though it's Saturday.

Two and a half weeks.

When I first found out that they were actually moving, I had five weeks to get used to the idea. Now the time is half gone.

Justin won't even talk to me about the fact that he's leaving.

He keeps acting as if everything is the same.

I keep wanting to talk about it.

He won't.

It's driving me nuts.

Every time I mention it, he suggests we play or make something or watch a video.

Every time, I say, "Justin. I want to talk to you," he says, "I don't want to talk."

I don't know what to do.

Sometimes I think about talking to my mom about this but she's already really sad that the Danielses are leaving.

She and Mrs. Daniels have been friends since Justin and I were in preschool.

"Kids. I repeat, do me a favor and stay out of my way today," Mrs. Daniels says. "I've really got to get this stuff packed. I've put some boxes into your bedroom, Justin. I want you to go through all of your things. Throw out the things that are no good, broken. Put things that are still good but that you don't want in a box to give away to charity."

"Yea!" Justin yells.

His mother looks at him. "Justin Daniels. You are not going to try to give away that suit your grandmother sent you."

"Rats." Justin frowns.

"I'll help," I offer, wondering when I turned into the "Queen of Clean."

Heading into Justin and Danny's room, we step over already packed and labeled boxes.

Justin picks up a basketball and throws it at me.

I throw it back.

Soon we are playing a game of "Points for Hitting the Other Person."

We made the game up in second grade.

One point for a chest hit.

Two points for a direct hit to the rear end.

Three points for the big toe, the pinky, and the belly button.

You can lose points. You lose five points

if you hit the person in the head or in certain other places.

"Three points. Yes!" Justin smashes the ball into my shoe right where my big toe is.

Mrs. Daniels comes into the room. "And a minus twenty for you for not doing what I said. Look. We still have a lot to pack. I sent Danny over to his friend's house so that we could get more done. Now I'm treating you like a big boy, Justin. Please act like one."

Justin looks down at the floor.

I wonder. How come when adults say things like, "I'm treating you like a big boy or girl," you end up feeling like a baby.

She leaves and I say again, "I'll help."

We start going through the stuff in his closets.

In the important box go his baseball card collection, three blue ribbons from the county fair three-legged races (we always win those in our age group), his model airplanes and all of our school yearbooks.

"I'm going to throw this out. If my mother finds it she's going to have a fit." Justin holds up the chewing gum ball we have been adding to for a year and a half.

"But it's OURS. We both contributed to it." I think of all the times I was just going to throw the used gum out but instead I put it in a damp paper towel and then into a Baggie to keep it sticky so that we could put it on the ball.

Justin sighs and shrugs. "My mom is in a bad enough mood already."

"But it's OURS," I repeat.

"It's only a chewing gum ball." Justin sounds annoyed. "Amber. Why are you making such a big deal out of it?"

That does it.

Justin has gone too far.

"Throw it out and I'm never going to speak to you again." I stare at Justin.

He stares at me.

And then he picks up the ball, bends his

knees, and as if the chewing gum ball is a basketball, lobs it into the throw-out pile without saying a word.

I am never going to speak to Justin Daniels again.

Chapter Eight

It's not easy choosing a new best friend.

I sit on my bed, staring at the list of kids who are in my class.

First of all, it's going to take a long time to decide and then what if the person I choose already has a best friend or doesn't want me as a best friend.

The names are all written out in light blue ink. I am using a red pen to cross out all of the people who could never be my best friend. Alicia Sanchez and Naomi Schwartz are already best friends. So are Freddie Romano and Gregory Gifford. A couple of

the boys are very obnoxious so I've crossed them out. I would pick a slug with rabies before I would pick them. Hannah Burton is much too neat and cares too much about looking good. I could never be best friends with someone who has a list on her door of what she wears every day. She does that so that she never wears the same thing twice for at least two weeks. Once she had a pajama party at her house and I saw that her closet is color-coded and arranged by how long everything is—shirts, skirts, pants and dresses. She's a definite NO.

Brandi Colwin has a purple star by her name. She's a definite MAYBE. So is Marc Manchester.

Fredrich Allen, however, is an absolute NO. He's one of those pick-and-chew nose people.

There's a knock on my door. "Amber, honey. May I come in?"

I put the list under my pillow. "Sure."

My mother comes in, carrying a bowl and two spoons. I know that this is not nutritionally sound, and we shouldn't turn to food. But I can't help myself today."

She sits down on my bed.

Looking into the bowl, I say, "My favorite," as I see double fudge brownie mix with all of the ingredients, but unbaked.

"Thanks, Mom." I give her a hug.

"Promise me that for the rest of the week you'll take fruit to school for dessert." She holds back the spoon.

"I promise."

She hands the spoon over.

We both eat out of the bowl for a while and then my mother says, "Amber. I want to talk with you."

There's no such thing as a free brownie mix, I think.

She continues. "What's going on between you and Justin? Why have you two stopped talking?"

How do I tell her about the chewing gum ball, how he won't talk to me about leaving,

how he acts as if going away is one of the easiest things in the world.

I shake my head.

If I start to talk about it, I'll start to cry.

My mother puts the bowl and spoons on my desk and puts her arms around me.

"Amber." She kisses the top of my head.

I don't pull away when she does that although I usually do when she does it in front of other people.

"Amber." She kisses the top of my head again. "I know that you are going to miss

Justin. The two of you have a very special friendship."

"Not anymore, we don't," I say, starting to sniffle. "He's a jerk, a total and absolute jerk."

She continues. "It's hard when people leave you. Sometimes, even though it's not your fault, you think it is."

"I hate him." The tears start even though I don't want them to.

"No, you don't." My mother looks at me. "Honey, you're very angry now, but you know that Justin is your friend."

"He is not," I say.

"So tell me what's going on." She smooths my hair. "It'll be easier if you can talk about it."

I shake my head.

Continuing to smooth my hair, she says, "Sometimes when people have to leave each other, they act as if it isn't happening or they pick a fight so it won't seem so hard to go. In this case, it looks like both. But think of all the good times you and Justin are missing right now because you've stopped talking."

I start to cry more.

I hate to cry.

Sometimes I'm afraid that if I start, I'll never stop.

And now I've started.

My mother hugs me.

She hugs.

I cry.

We sit for a while and then I back away. "Mr. Cohen says that our bodies are made up of 80 percent liquid. The way I've been crying, the Weather Bureau could call me a drought. Thanks for the hug, Mom," I say. "I'll be okay now."

"Do you want to be alone?" she asks.

I nod.

"I'll be in the living room if you need

me." She gives me one more hug and then walks out.

I stare at her as she leaves.

I'm so lucky to have a mother who doesn't act like my feelings don't count, just because I'm a kid.

I take out my list and look at it.

Then I rip it up.

Getting a best friend isn't like making a shopping list.

I take Justin's school picture out of the drawer by my bed.

It's a little messy since I drew a black eye on him and used the red pen to give him chicken pox.

I look at the picture for a while and think.... He's going to miss me. Who else is going to whisper the correct word to him in reading group? Who else is going to make faces when some goofy grown-up says, "So your name is Justin, like in the song 'Justin

Time'?" Who else is going to give up her cookie wafers for him? Cheer for him even when he strikes out? Who else is going to convince Danny that it's "Big Boy" to make his brother's bed for him?

I'll tell you something.

He's going to miss me.

I'll tell you something else.

I'm going to miss him.

Chapter
Nine

Today, Mr. Cohen's class is going to have a pizza party.

That's the good news.

The bad news is that it's a going-away party for my ex-best friend, Justin Daniels, and we still haven't spoken to each other.

I've been waiting for him to say "I'm sorry."

I don't know what he's been waiting for.

So we've been sitting in class right next to each other without saying a word.

Well, hardly a word.

I confess. Once I did say, "Hey, dirt bag.

Would you please pass the eraser?"

And he said, "Crayon brain, get your own eraser."

It hurts a lot but I'm not going to give in on this one.

Justin is just so stubborn.

Today, the class "returned" from our trip to China.

Next we'll be "going" to Australia.

I can't wait.

Justin, however, won't be "going." He'll be going to Alabama for real.

I wish Al Abama was a real person so I could tell him how much I hate him.

As Brandi Colwin walks by our desks, I call out, "Hey, Brandi. Don't forget. We're going to sit next to each other when we go to Australia."

Then Justin turns to Hannah and says, "I'll be sure to send you some postcards from Alabama."

I yawn, a big yawn, right in his face, to

show I don't care, and then I pretend to scrunch up over my worksheet so that he can't see that I'm very close to crying.

Mr. Cohen flicks the lights off and on. "The pizza will be here in five minutes. Extra cheese, mushrooms, the works."

I pick up my head and look over at Justin.

He doesn't look any happier that I feel.

I make a decision and call out, "Tell the guy to hold the anchovies," and then look right at Justin, pretending to be holding wiggly anchovies.

He starts to laugh.

I pretend to flip an anchovy over to him.

He pretends to grab it.

"Let's go stand in the hall for a minute," Justin says, picking up his knapsack.

We both walk over to Mr. Cohen and ask to go out in the hall for a few minutes.

"Sure." He motions to the door.

As we walk out, I think I hear Mr. Cohen say, "Finally."

Once we get out there, we just stand quietly for a few minutes.

Then we both say "I'm sorry" at the same time and link pinkies.

"I don't want you to go." I start to cry, just a little.

Justin takes a deep breath and says, "I don't want to go either. You think this is easy? My new school is so big. I don't know anyone there. What if I forget my locker combination? All the kids there already

know each other. My parents say I have to be brave, to be a good example for Danny. That it will be fun. But I know my mom is nervous about moving, too. I heard her talking to your mom. And it's too late to join a little league team, and everyone there thinks I talk funny and I have to learn to say 'Y'all' and 'Ma'am,' and . . . and . . ."

I say, "And?"

Justin turns red. "And I'm going to miss you."

I smile for what seems like the first time in years.

We stand for a few minutes and then I say, "Why didn't you tell me that sooner?"

"Because you stopped talking to me," he says.

"You wouldn't talk to me." I defend myself. "Not about the important stuff."

"It's hard." He looks down at his untied shoelaces.

I say, "I want you to stay."

Justin looks up. "Me, too. But I can't. My parents are making me go. But they said you and your mom could visit this summer."

This summer. I better start practicing "Y'all" and "Ma'am."

Justin pulls something out of his knapsack.

It's a badly wrapped present.

I open the package.

It's a tissue box.

Inside the tissue box is the chewing gum ball.

"Thanks. It's the best present ever," I say,

knowing that I will save it for the rest of my life.

The pizza guy arrives with ten pizzas. My stomach smells the extra cheese. Mr. Cohen comes out.

"You two better get inside before everyone eats up all of this pizza. It's your party,
Justin."

As we walk inside, I think about how it
will be when Justin and I grow up and he
doesn't have to move just because his parents move.

Maybe someday we can open our own
company. I'll be president one week and
he'll be president the next. We'll sell jars of
icing and boxes of cookies.

Maybe someday we'll travel around the

world trying out new flavors of chewing gum, and the chewing gum ball will get so big that we'll build a house for it.

Until then, maybe, I can save some of my allowance each week and call Justin once in a while. He can do the same.

I think I'm going to learn his new phone number by heart.

Whenever I think about third grade, I'm going to think about Justin, and I bet he's always going to think about me.